undead folk

advanced praise for *undead folk*

"A beautiful, powerful and deeply original rendering of grief..." - Ross Jeffery, Bram Stoker Award-nominated author of *I Died Too, But They Haven't Buried Me Yet* and *The Devil's Pocketbook*

"With gut-wrenching situations, heartbreaking emotion, dynamic characters and concepts, Silva quickly engages and captivates her reader, with every word bled onto the pages..." - Candace Nola, author of *Desperate Wishes*

"*Undead Folk* is a unique exploration of grief and revenge told against a hauntingly beautiful post-apocalyptic backdrop. A short and powerful tale of loss, and the desolation and desperation that follows."
- Red Lagoe, author of *In Excess of Dark*

undead folk

by

katherine silva

SWP

Published by Strange Wilds Press
Print first edition: April 12th, 2024
Ebook first edition: May 1st, 2024

Cover design © Katherine Silva
www.katherinesilvaauthor.com
Strange Wilds Press Logo by MartaLeo
Cover photos courtesy of Pexels and Unsplash

ONE

Twilight trickled in like time in tedium: in delicate particles of nonentity. Time meant practically nothing anymore; not for the people of this place. There was nothing to look forward to and nothing to wait for... The steady drip-drop of existence ambled on with the rise and fall of the celestial bodies in the sky.

The train shuddered in on rusted rails, scraping and billowing black smoke into the air with its arrival. No one stirred to meet it as it did not stop. It merely passed through and no one knew where it unloaded. No one really cared.

A single person exited a cargo car on the low point before the bridge that crossed the river. Her body tumbled down the shale-lined hill into wilted Queen Anne's Lace.

She collected her sack from the dust, checked her pockets for her essentials and hiked the half mile down the nearest dirt road, following tire tracks that hadn't ground the dirt in near a decade. She hadn't seen a working car in a long time and she figured no one in the dried-up spit of a town owned or drove one either.

She was wrong.

The grass regained some of its color as she approached

the bog and with it, essences of life flitted about like the dirt clouds at her back. Crows called to one another across an open field. The casual meeps of frogs chimed in as the sun dropped low on the horizon. And then, she came across it: the bedraggled corpse of an animal cascaded to the side of the lane. Blood matted like strawberry jam in patches along its dried-out, bony hide. A fox, at least it had been at some point, and it had been run over by a car.

A sign: she was where she was supposed to be.

She knelt, dug into her pack until she found her heavy duty work gloves and donned them. She grabbed the fox's legs together in a bundle. Its body crackled in her fingers as she carried it the rest of the way down the lane to the abandoned house there.

Night plummeted and the temperature along with it. Cool blue overtook the shell of a home as she set the corpse down in the remains of the living room, as she checked the cabinets absently for left behind canned goods and came up empty. They were a luxury if they could be found at all. Though she had known she'd find none here, she still looked out of responsibility. Maybe for the nostalgia, too.

The pond in the back had shrunken since she'd last seen it. Nothing more than a shallow dip in the lawn, fed by the ribbon of a desiccated creek that undulated into the trees beyond the old yard. She scooped a swallow of water into a mug that said "Number One Dad!" and returned to the living room.

She lit candles: fingers of light in the coming darkness that she arranged about the room, not sporadically but with intention. From her bag, she gathered pouches of dried herbs and flowers, a half empty vial of clear liquid that she held close to her for a moment and breathed in despite there being no scent to it. She combined them all in the mug of almost pond water.

She recited memorized words from the jagged letters tattooed around her forearm by a kid in New Amsterdam. The red swelling around each one was beyond her concern now. There were more important matters at hand.

When she finished speaking, she poured a dollop out onto the withered fox corpse and the rest, she drank. Briny, sharp, smoldering on her tongue and down her throat. She never got used to the taste.

Then, she blew out the candles and nuzzled up onto the couch beneath the broken front room window to sleep. The chill seeped through her suede coat, through her sweater and the two layers beneath it. She wished she hadn't left her sleeping bag behind at the last place. But she'd had to leave. It was a sacrifice. Each one hurt less and less as the days dragged on.

TWO

His voice awoke her with the crispness of early morning.

"Goodness gravy," he croaked. "Um, excuse me? 'Scuse me? Are you okay?"

Fuck. She knew what would happen but every time a whisker of dread caressed her brain when she heard the voice. As she turned over, she took in the cracked ceiling, the crumbling plaster on the walls, the thick scent of late spring wildflowers that wafted in through the window.

"My god, what if she's dead? No, she isn't dead. She's *moving*. You've just got to raise your voice. HELLO? MA'AM? (Oof, she's not *that* old.) ARE YOU OKAY?"

"Don't call me 'ma'am.'" She grunted and sat up.

Before her, the corpse of the fox stood upright. An approximation of life filled its chest, colored its milky eyes and animated its bony limbs. It picked up one of its paws and held it in the air limply. "Sorry. That was not a reflection of your age. I knew I shouldn't have said it. But, that's beside the point. I asked if you were okay?"

"At least I'm breathing," she answered, collecting the candles from around the room and stuffing them in her bag.

Her stomach rattled emptily.

The fox cocked its head. "Okay. The reason I ask is because the house we're in looks pretty fucked up. Like someone committed an armed robbery and then maybe a triple homicide happened and then after a few years of rumors milling around town, a bunch of kids had a rager-party in it."

She almost laughed but the sound caught in her throat before it could leave her mouth. "No rager-parties here, Amos." After a final check that she had everything with her, she left the house.

"Hang on!" His voice chirped up from behind her. "God, it feels like I'm drunk. Heh. Um…I don't remember drinking but I must have. I can't get off my hands and knees…"

"You don't have hands or knees!" she yelled over her shoulder.

"I'm…" The voice went silent behind her. She stopped. The gravel and dirt crunched beneath her boots as she shifted to look back at the house. A twinge of pity hit her as she waited for Amos to say something; anything.

Moments later, the fox trotted through the open door and out onto the path behind her. "I think I wanted to be upset about that. But oddly, I'm not. I have a feeling you know why." He tilted his head up at her.

Judgement: it wasn't the first time she'd witnessed it from an undead creature. They all had regarded her with vacant eyes as strings of bloody saliva hung from their moldered mouths. They wanted answers she couldn't give them. No, she could. But each time she did, it carved a jagged sliver out of her. What was the point in education when they never remembered?

"You're dead, Amos." The words were clipped of any

emotion. "And I needed to bring you back. This was the only body I could find. Don't get existential on me." She turned around and kept walking.

Muttering behind her followed by the pat-pat of paws on the gravel. "No, Amos, don't ask any illuminating questions about your reanimation. Just accept the fact that this girl is a necromancer and that magic is real! Sure!" He caught up with her. "I am starting to think I've done mushrooms or something. Or Mescaline? Is that something you can get easily around here?"

"No. You're about a thousand miles away from finding any peyote."

She hiked over washed out crags in the dirt road. It seemed to be taking forever to find her way back to the railroad tracks. But it always was a longer path than she remembered when she came back here and Amos's unending diatribe made it significantly longer.

"So, I'm dead," he said. "How did I...Hmm. Maybe I don't really want to know."

"I wasn't there," she said. "But I heard it was quick."

"Guess that's better than a grueling, torturous end. Like starving. Or bleeding out."

She grit her teeth. "Look at you: thinking on the bright side."

"Listen—" He scuttled in front of her. "What do I call you anyway? My resurrectionist?"

"You don't need to know my name." She took a step.

He bounced to block her. "Well, we've already established that you hate 'ma'am'. Does this mean I get to pick? How about: Barbarella! No? Not even sure you know what that's from."

"It's from *Barbarella*."

The fox sniffed. "Points for you. I knew you were smarter than you looked."

She stepped over its minute figure and walked on. "Don't fucking call me 'Barbarella.'"

"Fine! How about: Dirty Harry? Too masculine for you? I know! I know: Dammit Janet?" He giggled. "That's my favorite so far."

She exhaled. "I can always take it back, you know? Turn you into a heap of bones again?"

"But what would be the fun in that!" When she looked back, she could almost see a smile on the fox's panting lips. "No, you need me for some reason, Dammit Janet, and I don't think me irritating you is enough to change your mind, is it?"

How she wanted to prove him wrong. But then she'd have to go back to the house and do the ritual all over again. A waste of her time. This was supposed to be the last time anyway.

"Last chance to be involved in choosing what I call you?"

She kept walking.

"Going once, going twice... SOLD to Dammit Janet!"

The railroad tracks appeared in the distance over a small hill. Only twenty minutes or so had passed, but the day had already gotten considerably warmer out and her skin glistened with sweat from it. It was only another couple hours or so until they got into town, until she could find food, until she could prepare for what needed to be done.

This time of the year, back when things were greener, mosquitos and blackflies were a constant presence. She'd played out on the lawn near the pond and returned to the house with welts that itched and turned near purple overnight. But the pond was a portal: part of the kingdom where her fantasies molded and shifted in childhood and even the nasty bites of insects couldn't sway her from her daily playtime at its edge. Now, there wasn't enough water for mosquitos to breed and their absence brought an uncomfortable stillness to the land as she walked.

The fox stopped next to a spot in the road and stared at it. "This smells…familiar," Amos murmured, as if to himself. But whatever he said, she heard. Part of the ritual. His voice didn't so much as leave his lips as it did travel in her thoughts like a memory.

"That's where I found your current body," she said.

He shrunk away from it. "It's a strange feeling. I almost *hear* it: the dirt. Does that make any sense?"

"I call it a grounding spot. Whenever I bring an animal back, they have a connection to where they died. The fox's blood seeped into the earth here. A part of you will always be a part of it."

"But *I'm* not it," Amos said. "I'm someone else in *its* body. Shouldn't I have a connection to where *I* actually died?"

Something had edged into his voice that she remembered all too well: panic. The first few times she'd tried the ritual, that panic had sprouted and flourished into rampant terror. Those animals had torn themselves apart contemplating their own realities. She'd perfected the ritual from then on: less of one herb, more of another; more pond water, less of the one from her vials. Less self-awareness, but more authenticity. Each subsequent reanimation reminded her more of what she came here to do. She'd sacrificed her own mental comfort for theirs if only to make sure a ritual didn't end in a flurry of torn feathers or fur.

She didn't want that for this fox either. "No. That's not how it works. Bodies have attachments to the earth. They become part of its cycle as they break down. Souls: the kinds I bring back, are like copies of the person left behind when they die. All they have are vague memories of their lives before."

His head snapped up to her. "What?"

"You're like a recording of Amos. Like I burned you onto a CD from a hard drive. Or I recorded you onto a videotape with a camera. You understand? You're not really him."

Amos sat and returned his sights to the spot on the road. "Oh…okay. I suppose that's good then. Especially if he's in heaven or something."

She scoffed. "Take one look at me and tell me you think I can tear souls out of the afterlife with a KFC recipe?"

"When you put it that way, it does sound ridiculous," he agreed.

The duo continued on their way.

THREE

No one maintained the railroad. Not even the railway service who sent trains back and forth from one beyond into another. It had been seven years since the world had stopped caring about maintaining pavement, clearing tracks, fixing buildings, and whatever other upkeep needed to happen to make sure people had places to thrive. No one *thrived* anymore: they existed. One day to the next.

The only reason the railroad stayed clear was because of the trains. Nothing short of a school bus on the tracks was going to dislodge a train and anything that got in its way was prime to be cut down or snuffed out under the weight of its pitching carriages.

Evidence of this pricked her attention as she walked: splinters of wood from downed saplings, halves of skeletons discarded into the weeds, trash and barrels and all manner of human refuse littered the track for miles and miles.

No one to clean up the earth. No one to care about coexistence, sustainability, or anything that might potentially heal the open sore of this world. Just an accumulation of railway flotsam and jetsam.

Amos had talked and talked and talked. When she

didn't respond, he monologued. Not about anything in particular either. The entire time he talked, she wondered what ratio she'd screwed up in the ritual that had made him want to free his mind any time a thought entered it. Maybe she'd used too much pond water after all? A couple of times, she contemplated ending his unlife with a swift kick to the skull. Go back. Find a different corpse. Do it all over again. This time, she'd get it right...

But this one was also the least fatalistic of her resurrected creatures. Amos felt sincere for something conjured in a ritual: for a copy. There was a nostalgia to his conversation that tickled at her, even if she didn't partake in it. Her mind wanted more of its cheeriness, more of its normality even if the driven side of her brain protested it.

"Ooh, you know what I miss?" he said as he loped at her heels. "Peas and carrots."

The words made her almost stop walking.

"I know: you probably thought I was going to say pizza or a cheeseburger or something heartily American like that. But, peas and carrots. Just something about them..."

"Don't you ever shut up?" she growled.

"You know, for someone who went out of their way to copy a soul and fuse it into a corpse, I originally thought you'd done it out of loneliness. Not anymore. You've been mean to me ever since I woke up."

"I didn't expect you to be this talkative."

The fox stopped. "Were you hoping for the soul of a mime or something?"

She looked back at him. "No."

"Well then, you'll just have to learn to give a little back.

After all, we're spending time together, aren't we…Janet?"

The words made her feel juvenile. All at once, she was back in kindergarten, crying under a table because another kid wouldn't let her use their markers. She hadn't said "please" when she'd asked. The refusal had snapped something in her brain as flimsy as a nail file. Others hadn't had to ask, had they? Why had she?

Her father had come to pick her up and take her home. Shortly after, they decided to homeschool her.

She squeezed her eyes shut. "I don't have time to play twenty questions with you, Amos."

"Why?" His voice was ever-patient. "Where exactly are we going?"

To tell him or not to tell him…

Not.

"To town."

"Ooh, the mysterious 'town.' Is 'town' inhabited by people who speak? Because then maybe I'll find someone to have a conversation with and you can get on with whatever mopey chore you have while I amuse myself."

Her shoulders stiffened and she resisted the urge to turn around and scream at him. More nostalgia fizzed up into her head as she tried to ram it back down.

"How did you know my name, Janet?" There was no venom behind the question as there had been the previous statement. Only curiosity.

The edges of her face prickled with numbness. She tried to focus on the tracks. "It was there in my head when I woke up. I just knew it."

"Then, we didn't know each other? From before?" The

fox kept pace with her. "I wasn't an uncle or your dad or something?"

She stopped in mid-stride and inhaled a quivering breath. Everything around them seemed to pause. The birds in the sky, the wind, the crickets in the tall grass…

She exhaled. "My dad's name was Hugh. He starved to death." Her words and breath were stolen in a gust of warm wind that swept under her jacket and hugged her skinny frame before it departed. But she knew he'd heard.

They stared at one another. She thought she saw the fox's eyes dim a little though it could have been refraction from the clouds overhead. They were opaque: no moisture or oxygen moving through them.

"I'm sorry," Amos said finally. Again: so genuine sounding, this copy.

It caught her off-guard. "Whatever. Let's keep going."

FOUR

She'd dreaded the old tunnel since before she'd left the cargo car of her train. She'd thought about ignoring the ritual, ignoring the house and just riding it until she was passed it. But she needed Amos. And while the faint thought of waiting to catch another train to ride had seemed tempting, she wasn't sure when the next one would pass through. It wasn't as if they had schedules anymore.

The silence from their previous conversation had bled into the surrounding landscape. The birds had stopped their squawking. Even the crickets had quieted their songs as the two of them neared the turn in the track before the old tunnel.

Amos kept his head low and padded along beside her without comment. She took his quietness for fear. The revisiting of old wounds, of making her uncomfortable... It should have been considerate but it made her blood singe beneath her skin. Avoidance wasn't a gift. That wasn't the whole point of this trip at all. While she'd been angry about Hugh resurfacing in her thoughts, she was grateful for the calm it brought her.

Her Dad.

The one who brought her gifts from the yard: sweet clovers to chew on, blackberries to smash into jam, seeds to plant, and rocks to rub the dirt from and admire how they sparkled. How they slept under the stars in their backyard and traced the constellations with their fingers. How they pressed flowers between pages and followed animal tracks through the soft patches of mud in spring that led them into the woods. How they—

"What's that?"

Snagged in the threads of her thoughts, she looked down at Amos. He'd stopped a little behind her. The mouth of the old tunnel stared back at them from ahead: its darkness vast. It seemed to tug at the edges of her thoughts: little fragments of her memories with Hugh sifting away like sand in the receding tide.

Hungry.

"An old train tunnel. It's short. We'll be through it in no time." Even as she made herself keep walking, she knew her steps were smaller and her breath came in shorter inhales than before. She couldn't see the other side, but the refraction of morning light played on the far wall inside where it turned the corner. About a hundred yards or so of darkness, of saturating cold, and hopefully nothing more than that.

"Isn't there another way around, maybe?" Amos asked, a jitter in his voice.

"No." There was, but it would cost them a day and she didn't have that kind of time.

His paws shuffled in the ballast as he joined her once

more.

Her hand hovered over her hip where her only weapon hung in her dad's old tool belt: a rusted, heavy-headed adjustable wrench. It had been some time since she'd had to actually wield it. It had scared off more than a few vultures who had tried to steal from her in the past.

They entered the shadow of the mountain and then shortly after, the entrance and its dank interior loomed over their tiny figures. Swinging off her pack, she produced a large lantern flashlight combo and turned it on. Its white neon beam pierced the dark but was swallowed by the pit further inside.

"Good. You have a light. I was about to be worried," Amos chuckled. "Let's get this over with, shall we?"

"Not a fan of the dark, Amos?"

"No. It makes my skin crawl."

"That could be the maggots."

"Oh...right."

They walked further inside. She ran the light across the concaved stone walls inside. She used to know every inch of this tunnel; had run its length up and down like it was a playground when she was a girl. Then, the train had a schedule and they were never in the tunnel when the trains were running. But at nights, when service stopped, it became safe and they weren't the only ones using it for refuge against the elements.

Debris from old campsites lingered on the sides of the tracks: old tarps shorn to shreds, tents with snapped poles, discarded and empty boxes and cans of non-perishables. She paused in front of one particular spot where a faded and dirty tent footprint lay wrinkled beneath a collection of old fleeces, the glimmer of a space blanket catching against her flashlight's glow.

"What a horrible way to live," Amos said.

She didn't let the comment stick. Instead, she leaned down and pawed through the remains of the blankets until she found a little crushed match box. Inside were a collection of pebbles, curled up husks of fiddleheads, and a tiny plastic figurine of a fox.

Her mementos. They'd somehow survived all this time.

"Shine your light over here, would you?"

She did. A note was scratched into one of the rocks just to her left.

" 'A plus H,'" Amos read distantly. "Huh."

The scratch of the rocks still resounded in her head from when she'd carved it. Her dad had gone down to the end of the tunnel to try and barter with one of the other families there, but had returned empty-handed. When he saw her carving, he gave her a meek smile and told her they had to walk into town for food. They had never come back to this spot.

She stood, skin bristling as a shuffling sound echoed up from the chasm of darkness before them.

Amos snapped to attention. "What's that?"

"Probably just the wind," she muttered, though her fingers rested on the head of her wrench. "Let's keep going." She tucked the match box into the pocket of her coat.

"Are you sure?"

She kept walking.

They reached the halfway point of the tunnel. She kept

her eyes on the emerging light from the bend ahead. No one would be stupid enough to stay out here this far from town, she told herself. There was nothing to scavenge out here anymore. All the homes had been picked clean. All the animals could either outrun or out-fly even the healthiest of people. There were no guns. There was no ammunition to speak of here.

Amos's voice chirped up. "What happened?"

"What happened with what?"

"To this place."

She knew the ritual brought back copies with blanks in their memories. It was odd; the details some of the others recalled. Not a one had recognized the carnage or the desolation. Still, she tested him. "You don't remember?"

"No."

"I'll tell you when we get out of here."

"That's fair."

The light poured further along the tunnel wall as they drew closer to the exit. She exhaled, thumbed the match box in her pocket, the trinkets shaking inside like a box of Reese's Pieces. It had been so long since she'd had those. Her father used to get them for her before everything—

Something lunged from the blackness. Fingers buried themselves against her chest as she stumbled and collapsed under the weight. Her flashlight tumbled away into the dark. Her arm was caught under her as she tried to raise her head to see what was going on.

Knuckles slammed into her eye and dredged her head in the peastones near the track.

"Give!" someone screamed: a sound as dried out as the

world, as liminal as the tunnel around her. "I know you've got something. I saw you take it!" The fist struck her jaw and the taste of iron trickled over her lips, pooling in the hollow beneath her tongue.

She spat blood and yelled Amos's name as she struggled to get her arm out from beneath her. Her other one tried to protect her face from another blow. The darkness swam like schools of frightened fish in her vision, lurching this way and that. Her wrist ground into the ballast as she curled her fingers around the head of her wrench.

Greedy hands scrabbled at her matchbox as she squirmed. A boot came down on her thigh like bricks and she squealed. "I knew it! I knew you had something!" They tore the matchbox from her pocket.

Grabbing a handful of stones, she threw them into the attacker's face. They cried and tried to shield themselves. Then, she kicked as hard as she could, the heel of her boot ramming into their knee with a sickening crack.

They crumpled next to her with a howl.

Wriggling up into a sitting position, she yanked the wrench from her tool belt and swung it backhanded, connecting with something, something that made the metal sing through her hand, up her arm, all the way to her jaw...

Screaming, crying. The man or woman or whoever floundered on the tracks, flinging stones left and right as they spasmed. She got to her knees. The sharp edges of stones nestled into her bony shins as she brought he wrench up and back down. Soft thuds soon turned to squelches, then turned to crunches. She pushed all the sound out of her lungs because it drowned out the noise; reminded her she wasn't abandoned like the rest of the world, not yet anyway.

The wrench slipped from her fingers before she could bring it down again. It banged across the tracks, pinging into the shadows beyond as she slumped. Blood thundered in her head and neck. Her hands were slick with gore: what kind she didn't care to know. She stood and her entire body leaned to one side as gravity reminded her of its presence. Her leg throbbed. She spat a gob of blood from her mouth and rubbed her tongue along her teeth. Nothing broken. Nothing cracked by the feel.

Purple sparks of pain ignited in her right eye. They'd gotten her good whoever they were, whatever the years made them become. She retrieved the flashlight from where it had landed and searched the carnage for her matchbox.

Think of asters. Think of daisies. Think of cosmos. Her father's words echoed in her head as she located the box, flattened under the assailant's boot. She picked what individual rocks she could find, the ferns, the bits of sea glass, and the fox and shoved them into her pocket.

"Amos?" she called into the darkness, swinging the light left, then right. He didn't answer.

She trudged the rest of the way out of the tunnel. The sun bathed her in its hot sheen; the wind drying her sweat and the blood. She found the fox cowering around the corner, curled in a fetal position. "It's over," she said.

It took a moment for the animal to see her, then really see her. "Oh my god…"

"You fucking ran?"

"I…I was scared," Amos blubbered.

"You're already dead." She should have been furious. But she'd expected it. Amos wasn't a fighter. Never had been. Never would be.

"You killed them?" More firmly. "You killed them."

"Had to. Did you want me to die?"

"No." The corner of the fox's lip curled. "But I—"

"Then yeah. I did what I had to do." She turned away from him.

"I don't even know you!" he snapped. "I have no idea what the hell is even going on!"

"I told you I'd tell you once we got out of the cave." She sniffed and glanced down the tracks. It was another hour until they reached town. While she hated to walk that far caked in human blood, she knew she had no other options. No options other than…

No. She swore she'd never go back there. Even if it had running water. Even if it was a weird safe haven in the middle of a dissolving town. It held a desolation that was all consuming and made the corners of her brain twitch with persuasive inklings of fear.

The fox just stared at her and Amos said nothing.

She looked down at her hands. She *couldn't* go into town like this. She couldn't afford to stick out. She had to blend in and not be noticed. Which meant she'd *have* to clean up first. She had to go *there*.

Parting from the tracks, she set off into the field nearby on a path filled in by golden rod and wheatgrass over the years. She turned to look behind her. The fox had come to the edge of the ballast and watched her.

"What are you going to do by yourself?" she asked.

"Come on."

Soon enough, she heard him shuffling through the grass behind her. "Tell me," he said quietly. "Tell me everything."

FIVE

People always wanted more than they had. Once they had those things, the lesser things were left behind, discarded, and forgotten. When people could no longer sustain the place they'd called home for centuries, for millennia: they came up with a solution. They would escape it. And so, they did. The wealthy ones. The ones with the right political alignments. The ones who had friends in high places: either religiously or literally.

The discarded ones were split. Those who took power because they could, did so with selfish abandon. They weren't looking to better the failing world for their fellow men and women. They were looking to be buried with their diamonds and sneaker collections and all the toilet paper on the eastern seaboard in the grandiose homes they'd claimed for their own. Opportunistic scavengers aligned with them for a piece of the pie, determined to do whatever it took to earn the prosperity their masters had stolen for themselves.

What was left: the dregs. The already beaten down. The poor. The ones with no connections. The barely scraping by. The unlucky ones.

She told all of this to Amos as they traipsed the path further into the field, as she swept grass out of her way and tried to ignore the worsening bang of a headache behind her black eye. They weren't far off now. But the thought of being near it, the memory of its white empty halls and white empty rooms, and the empty people who'd lived inside of it was like swallowing expired milk.

"So," Amos finally said. "You were unlucky?"

"My parents lived off the grid away from town. They chose to live unconventionally because the conventional world had never done right by them. Initially, when things went to hell, we were ready for it. We had a full garden, a place to hunt for wild game, chickens for eggs... But they didn't count on the drought. And..."

Her voice drifted off as she noticed the glimmer of windows in the distance. The white building sat in the midst of the field like a beacon, waves of heat making its walls ripple before them like a mirage. Its spacious parking lot was devoid of cars. It was as though someone had dropped it in the middle of the hills and then forgot about it.

"Is that..." Amos started to ask. "...A car dealership?"

She scoffed and shook her head. It had that look. Boxy and ugly, with large windows that looked like they should be showing off a brand new Ferrari or Porsche on a rotating platform. But the outside of the place was vacant of any signage to explain what it really was. Few people knew about it years ago. It was probably why no one had come to look for it miles outside of town, miles out from the railroad. At least: she hoped no one had.

The sound of her boots meeting the old pavement was a

strange one after spending so much time on loose rock and trails. The fox's claws clicked on the hardtop as he followed her through the parking lot toward the front entrance.

They stopped about ten feet from the doors. A nervous tremor zinged up and down her back as she tried to will herself on.

"Well?" The fox rounded her. "Are we going in?"

"You should stay out here."

"Let me guess: they don't allow animals?" The fox cocked its head. "Aren't we in some kind of an apocalypse situation? You'd think they'd be okay with a zombified canine."

His comment barely made a dent. It was as though she could smell those halls all over again: a disinfected alcoholic odor so pungent, it sat itself in the base of her stomach and occasionally tickled the back of her throat. "I think you should stay outside."

This time, he didn't return a snarky comment. When she looked down at him, he was lying down, resting his muzzle on his front legs. "Are you sure you should go inside?"

No. She wasn't. But if she wanted to do this; really do this, it was a sacrifice she had to make. And she'd known she couldn't avoid this place forever. Finality drew her closer to the doors. She curled her fingers around the metal pull bar and it soundlessly gave way under her strength. One step. Two steps…

The fox darted in around her feet and she nearly tripped over it. "Amos!"

"You're scared to be in here, Janet. I know it," he said and the fox glanced back over its shoulder at her. "I'll keep you company."

"Like you kept me company in the train tunnel?" Anger flashed in her words.

When the fox cocked its head this time, there was the audible crich-crunch of bones. "I won't leave you. I promise."

A waiting area sprawled around them with uncomfortable-looking brown-vinyl chairs. A cobweb-shrouded old television was tucked up in the corner near the ceiling and a coffee table in the center was splattered with magazines of every type: gardening, cooking, entertainment...

The fox neared a rack of dusty pamphlets and Amos read them. "'Choosing the right plan for your loved one.' 'Ten signs and symptoms to be conscious about.' Hmm...this one appears to be a coupon for one free pizza at Secundo's?"

Secundo's. She hadn't thought about that place in years. When she was small and they used to go into town often, her father would take her there. Gave her quarters to play the arcade games. Barbeque chicken pizza and root beer and that fun racing game that made her want to grow up and learn how to drive her dad's little Pontiac.

"A hospital?" The fox backed away from the card rack and padded over to the center of the waiting area. "Out here in the middle of nowhere? What a strange place."

"It's not a hospital," she answered, walking further in towards the reception desk. "It was a hospice house."

"*This?*" After a moment, Amos sighed. "I suppose it makes sense. This dodecahedron-looking art piece out in the middle of nowhere. It was some rich person's idea of a hospice house no doubt."

"My dad and I used to come here all the time to visit," she said and stared at her shoes.

"Ah," Amos said. "Your mother."

She didn't answer.

"You haven't talked about her at all. I guess I understand why you don't want to be here."

She shrugged.

"Let's make this quick then," he said.

She opened the door next to the reception desk into a long-carpeted hall. As they walked, the fuzzy feeling in her mouth started to take over the rest of her head. This place had never been full of life per say, but there had always been a presence here. People in scrubs passed them by whenever they had come. Fellow visitors and fellow patients, too. Now, like everywhere else, the silence reigned.

Passing a table with dried brown flowers in the vase, she gazed at the door to the stairwell. A nearby sign pointed to it and noted that patient rooms were upstairs.

"Come on," Amos prodded gently. "You don't have to, you know?"

But this was the point. The burying of the hatchet. The confrontation. It had taken her so long to chase her own tail around this godforsaken country and when she was finally done running, she realized that she could never outrun what had happened here. There was nothing to look forward to. Only to look back on.

She pushed open the stair door and ascended the steps.

A long hall greeted her on the next floor similar to the one they'd walked downstairs. The cream-colored carpet led her past an array of open doors all looking into copies of what seemed like the same room over and over. No personal effects inside. Nothing to distinguish them as one person's over another's. She was fairly certain that everyone's belongings had either ended up in a storage room in the basement or they were burned in a massive bonfire. Each room scraped of its identity. Spotless once more.

"It's so clean here," Amos remarked.

She didn't add any comment.

She stopped three-quarters of the way down the hall between two rooms and glanced from one door to the next. She couldn't remember which one they used to visit. It had been years.

The fox padded into the room on the left and toward the window that overlooked the mountainside. The deciduous trees budded with the new green of spring; the wildflowers in the field popped like colorful sprinkles in the grass. The sky had gone overcast but no rain would fall. It rarely did.

"Pretty view," he commented absently. "Very striking."

Her heart drummed in her chest and blood squelched in her ears.

The fox walked back to her. "Do you mind if I ask what happened to her?"

Her eyes drifted to the bed and she swallowed thickly. "It started with little things first: misplacing glasses, keys… that kind of stuff. Forgetting to close the front door. Forgetting the lyrics to a song we used to sing together all the time. Dad knew. He knew before I did. I think he tried to protect me from it until, well, it became unignorable."

"Dementia," Amos said.

She nodded. "Wandering came next. Dad and I would drive around looking. A field one time. A neighbor's front porch another time. By the train tracks the last time. It wasn't safe anymore. This place was the only option."

She remembered the early weeks. There was still life there. Cheer. Recognition. But it faded. And how quickly it faded as things deteriorated outside.

"When things went off, this place needed more money to stay going. Dad gave almost everything we had and it still wasn't enough. The land and the house though… Those were still valuable, then anyway. So, he sold them."

"Jesus…" Amos whispered.

"The neighbors had offered us a room in their house and we stayed until the electric grid went down. And that's when Dad got the call: that even the ludicrous amount of money he'd dropped in the hospice house's lap wasn't enough. It didn't mean anything anymore. This place couldn't continue to operate like it had. So…they made a choice."

"I don't like the sound of that…"

She remembered her dad buttoning a shirt that trembling hands couldn't remember how to, spooning broth into a mouth that sometimes didn't open because the memory of how to eat had lost permanence.

They left the room. With each step they descended, the weight of that room was replaced by tiny ball bearings of emotionlessness, each one settling into a larger pile deep in her chest. Once they were back on the ground floor, they continued through a heavy set of push open double-doors into the bathing area.

A fifteen-foot swimming pool stretched along the length of the room. A skim of dust rested on the surface of the still water. Beyond were the showers. But she passed the locker rooms by and instead, held her arm out to open the emergency exit door that led to the back of the facility.

Outside the air sat dead; not a breeze to muster the sand or to dance through the wildflowers. At the edge of the field, a row of crosses peeked up from the grass. Her gaze locked on the second to last one.

"They killed the patients?" Amos asked, knowingly.

"They thought it was better to put them out of their misery rather than let their quality of life dwindle into nothing."

"What happened to the others? The ones who worked here?"

"The guy who used to own this place lives in town now." A familiar toasty wrath warmed her cheeks. "Everyone else? You didn't look closely enough at the swimming pool, did you?"

If the fox wasn't already dead, she swore she would have seen its face pale. It sat and huffed in and out. "Dear god…"

"If only *he* actually cared," she muttered. They went back inside.

The fox stayed close to the wall and avoided looking toward the pool while she headed for the bathrooms. "Stay out here. I'm going to clean up."

Amos didn't have a chance to answer before she pushed through into the shiny, pink tiled room.

The showers lay toward the back past the toilets and the lockers. She ran the water in the sink first, yanked off her shirt and pumped hand soap into her palm to scrub away at the blood, the brain matter, the bits of bone. The water burned red, then blushed pink. The shirt would forever be stained. It didn't matter. As long as she could get close enough to Him, the rest would go as she'd planned.

Dropping the rest of her clothes, she bathed in the

shower. The hot water stung her skin: painful and pleasurable at the same time. How long had it been since she'd felt running water? A month?

While she showered, she took stock of her injuries. Her leg was bruised, the dark splotches patterned in angled dots and blips that eventually shaped into the heel of a boot. Her eye had swollen, but not shut thankfully, as had her lip. They tingled under the touch of her fingers as she tenderly poked at them.

Clean or somewhat clean. Cleaner than she'd been in a while at least. She put the wet t-shirt back on. It would dry in the sun.

When she left the locker room, the fox was curled up on one of the lounge chairs nearest the wall. She joined him, the canvas bowing under her as she sat. "Ready to go?"

"Yes." His voice was troubled. "How is there still running water here? And electricity?"

"Solar," she said nodding to the roof. "And water tanks up there, too. If this place wasn't so horrible, I could have stayed here."

They left the building. The heat baked her skin as they crossed the parking lot back toward the path that would return them to the train tracks.

"You've been really quiet," she observed.

"I've been remembering some things," Amos said. "But it's hard. It's like looking at someone else's photo album. Lots of faces. Lots of rooms and places maybe I should recognize. Every now and then, there's a flicker of something. I think…maybe I had a daughter."

Sweltering heat crowded in on her. The t-shirt stuck

to her bony figure, warm and uncomfortable. "You think?"

"I have little movements of her in my head. Brown hair. Brown eyes. This cute little nose but a very discerning gaze. It's like she's trying to choose her next chess move or something."

"Do you remember her name?"

The fox huffed. "No."

Probably for the best, she thought as they kept walking. Her mind was driven toward the tracks, toward the town but a sliver of her was curious. So far, the fox was the one who had recalled the most. Even the rattlesnake hadn't remembered a thing about its life before and that one had been with her for a solid forty-eight hours. If this was going to be the last one, maybe it was worth helping the process along?

She shoved the thought down as soon as it entered her mind. Things were going to end badly. This wasn't the time make connections. Detachment was key.

"She's singing," he said wistfully.

She looked down at the fox. "What?"

"In my memory, she's singing. I know the song…I just don't remember what it's called. I love this song. It makes me feel alive again."

She cleared her throat. "Train tracks are up ahead."

The return to the railroad brought her intention back full swing. Not much longer now. Anxiety leaked through her limbs, twitched down in her fingertips. There were only so many people in town but they all worked for the Man. He surrounded himself in human shields.

They'd have to enter under cover of darkness. And judging by where the sun was in the sky, it was afternoon…

maybe three o'clock? They'd have some time to kill beforehand, even with the detour they'd taken.

"Why are we going to town, Janet?" Amos asked.

"Because I have an errand to run."

"Must be some kind of errand. To endure that kind of an attack. To go to a place that brought back painful memories for you…"

"The alternative is death. I'd say it's important." She coughed into her sleeve. She already missed the water from the shower, the feeling of it running down her throat. Soon enough, she'd be in town. She'd get more.

"Are you going to town to see someone?"

Right to the point. She'd given him enough information, but she hadn't expected him to put it together. Hadn't wanted him to. "Sort of." She didn't want to lie to him anymore so this was the closest non-committal answer she could give.

"You mentioned that people took power when there was a vacancy and the unlucky ones got left behind? I'm guessing that town isn't run by the unlucky ones?"

She shook her head.

The fox loped ahead of her and sat in the middle of the tracks. "Is this a suicide mission?"

She stopped and regarded the fox, the bits of fur and flesh gnawed away on his muzzle, the sheen of bone that showed on one of his front legs… Was there something about the animal she'd chosen that had given Amos better intuition? Her father used to tell her foxes were clever. Or had her tincture for the ritual been so perfect that she'd managed the unthinkable: she'd really brought the real

Amos back? Back like he used to be...

"Janet?" The fox tilted its head.

She shook her head. "No. I don't plan on dying."

A moment of silence passed before Amos said, "Don't do anything stupid, Janet. I'm starting to really like you." With that, the fox turned and continued up the tracks.

She swallowed the boulder in her throat and followed.

The afternoon stretched and the sky cooled into lavender shades as they walked. Amos talked. He told her about the girl he thought might have been his daughter. His fleeting wisps of memory about her. They made paper stars together and hung them in her room. They sang. They watched old musicals and danced along with the characters in them. They plucked carrots from the soil and picked peapods.

"Peas and carrots," he muttered fondly.

And as he talked, she thought about her father. And she thought about how her dad had gradually lost his smile. How he missed his love but never spoke about it to her. How he withered as he gave her everything he had and more. How he made sure she stayed alive. How he thinned and grayed and his skin turned to paper and how that cold, overcast morning he had died before she'd even woken—

A screech pierced the orange sky.

Her hand went to her tool belt and prodded the empty place where her wrench used to sit. She'd left it behind in the tunnel.

The fox's head perked up, ears twitching. "What was that?"

It had almost sounded human. Almost.

She took a few steps forward, scanning the ground for a weapon of some kind. Ballast. The rusted railway. Grass.

The ribs from an animal skeleton.

"It sounded close," Amos added, padding back to her. "We should—"

Something sprung from the grass: a slender whip of shadow that tackled the fox with a scream. They writhed on the tracks in front of her: the fox keening wildly, Amos yelping, the thing howling.

"No!" The word burst from her throat as she scrambled toward them. Her fingers raked at the ballast and she flung a handful of it at the roiling fur and flesh.

The attacking creature swung toward her: dark fur bristled, eyes wild and shrieked at her. A fisher. She knew of them but had never seen one. It wriggled across the tracks faster than she'd seen anything move.

Instinct made her jump toward the drop off where the grass hugged the ballast.

The fisher's lithe form pivoted and latched onto her, claws burying in her leg as it tried to bite through the sleeve of her jacket.

She yelled, one arm protecting her body, the other prodding for something, anything...

"Janet!"

The fox barreled into the fisher, knocking it from her. They scuffled in the dirt, snarling and squealing. Soon the tearing of flesh. Amos crying.

She curled her fingers around a fist-sized rock and ran to the tumbling mass of growling animals. Rage roiled through her throat like hellfire as she swung her leg back and kicked as hard as she could, the toe of her boot connecting with its soft underbelly.

The fisher tumbled away with a snarl.

She flung the rock as hard as she could and it hit the animal in the side, the sound like meat smacking on concrete. It skittered away into the grass and she listened to its whimpers trail off toward the darkening horizon.

She dropped into the dirt next to the fox. "Amos?"

The soft breeze tickled the fox's fur on its torn open breast. The eyes had been scratched from their sockets, one dangling perilously across its moldered cheek. Amos didn't answer.

"Fuck!" She jumped to her feet. Anger was a thick, blinding cloud in her head. She ran to the bare animal skeleton, a deer once, and kicked it, shards of bone clinking and shattering with each connection. "Fuck! Fuuuuuuck!"

Warmth spilled across her cheeks as she collapsed against the earth. She hadn't cried in years. Not for any of the animals who had come before. Not even the rattlesnake.

Amos was gone.

Again.

SIX

Smokestacks on the horizon signaled the outskirts of town. The encampments were the last bastion of the unlucky ones: a collective of wanderers who broke apart and came together like a hive of bees. They'd scatter across the land, searching for things to trade to eke out a living. Sometimes, they had something valuable enough to warrant them a stay in town. A decadent meal. A hot bath. An actual bed.

She hadn't planned on stopping there for long. It was going to be where she'd planned to pass the time before she went into town. But now, Amos was gone and she needed to find a replacement.

Shop stalls were set up in rows: flimsy constructions that could be broken down and carted off quickly if need be. Some people used the backs of their old cars, wagons, and tents to show off their wares. Everything from old radios to cooking pots to automobile parts. The stench of old dust, of oil, of the woodsmoke from barrels around the encampment brought her back to the remainder of her childhood.

She didn't like being around so many people, but she knew no one in a place like this was going to start a fight or do anything that would get the attention of the town. The only reason that town let them stay was because there was occasionally something in it for them. The unlucky ones sometimes brought luxuries and when they bartered those luxuries, it benefited everyone.

She stopped at a tent where an old man had set out an array of shop tools, all oiled and glistening silver against the firelight. She bartered her tool belt for a new wrench which she tucked into her backpack.

Then, she searched for the taxidermist. She was a rare soul: one whose trade would normally have died out with the old world. But the nouveau riche still enjoyed trophies and she provided them.

She approached the dingy tent and drew back the opening. Inside, the woman lorded over the corpse of a raccoon. Her fingers made precise cuts with the knife; each rend of flesh painted the air with the horrid sound. The woman looked up. "It's been a while since you showed your face around here, Ella."

Ella approached the woman, arms extended with the corpse of the fox. "I brought you something."

The woman's nose scrunched. "I can't use that."

"Please."

"It's missing patches. It's old. People pay for the whole thing."

"The tail is still intact. People will pay good money for a fox tail."

The woman looked at her. "I suppose this isn't a gift. You want something in return?"

"What's on your to-do roster?" Ella asked.

The woman raised her eyebrows. "For a fox tail?" She

straightened and nibbled at a piece of jerky. "Only got one."

She led Ella back behind her table into the workshop: an old U-Haul van with the back doors open to reveal its interior. Furs lined the walls and a display of taxidermy animals stood to attention as the woman stepped up into the cavity by them: beavers, muskrats, squirrels, even a bobcat with fake eyes that seemed to glow.

The woman opened a cooler toward the back and reached inside. "Found this little guy up in the woods a bit north of here."

A marten. No fur missing. No bones showing. The woman had probably trapped and killed it herself. Some of the women in power liked cute pieces like this one. A fox tail wasn't any good unless someone was putting it on a hat or pretending it came out of their own ass for pleasure. Ella was getting a deal.

"He'll do."

The woman squinted. "'He?'"

"*It'll* do."

Ella retreated to the outskirts of the outskirts: close enough for the ruckus of them to be heard, for her campsite to merge with the smoke from the other, and for the wildlife to lose encouragement that she could offer a tasty morsel for them. Far enough away not to be bothered though.

A campfire from twigs and bits of wood scrounged near the railroad. A one-person tent with a broken pole she'd found in the garbage heap along with a tarp. It would do for however long it took to bring the marten back.

She set up the candles and lit them, their circle giving

her a faint sense of security even as the wind picked up. A storm was on the horizon. She felt the warm nip of it, the tang of electricity on the air.

Ella lay the marten down at the entrance of her tent and opened her bag. Her mouth dried. The bottle she'd kept her pond water in from the house was empty. At some point, the top had come off. It had leaked into her bag and dried. There was no connection to the house.

She needed moisture other than the vial. Something to infuse the other concoctions together. She had nothing left to trade in the outskirts, not even for a sip of water and she doubted the taxidermist would allow her anymore special treatment.

Ella arranged the herbs on the marten's body and hesitatingly poured the last of her vial of tears onto its soft coat. She'd have to hope for rain. It was all she had left: the wish for a miracle.

She spoke the memorized incantation. And then she spoke to the stars or where she imagined they would be if she could see past the clouds. "Dad. You didn't die for nothing. Everything comes full circle. I promise."

The candle flames flickered and eventually winnowed into darkness.

"Excuse me?"

Fat drops of rain pummeled her face. Ella opened her eyes.

"Ma'am? Ugh, she's not old enough to be called 'ma'am.' Hello?"

She sat up.

The marten shivered before her. Tiny black eyes shined as

they peered at her. "It's raining. May I come into your tent?"

Ella nodded and the creature shuffled inside. "God. What a storm, huh? It's so cold I can hardly move. Feels like I'm crawling."

"Go to sleep, Amos. It'll be morning in a few hours. You'll feel better then."

The marten yawned and curled up next to her. "Do I know you? I know you from somewhere, don't I?"

Words stuck in her throat. "I'm Janet."

He chuckled. "Janet. Like Dammit Janet? That's funny. Didn't think I knew any Janets." The marten drifted off to sleep.

SEVEN

Ella woke at three a.m. when the bells in town chimed. The storm had ended almost as soon as it began. She could have sworn she'd heard laughter as people in the outskirts raced to collect it in every vessel they had available. Her own jug was half-full now. She took a large swig and savored the gush of it in over her tongue.

The marten stirred. "Still dark. Why are you awake?"

"Because I have business to do, Amos."

"Business?" His voice was muddy with tire. "What kind of business?"

"A gratifying kind."

The marten blinked. "I don't know what that means."

"Get up and you'll see."

"I…" The marten stood on its tiny legs. "Well, this is as far as I can… Oh."

"You're dead, Amos. I found the body of a marten to put you into." She swallowed. "Don't get existential on me."

She packed up the tent, the candles, and the jug of water. The marten watched. Then, they started back toward the outskirts.

"You said your name was Janet?" he asked.

"I did."

"You remind me of someone else."

"Someone who?"

The marten ran to catch up with her. "I don't remember."

They passed through the muddy canals between shops, the only sound belonging to the soft snores and whistles of those still asleep. Water plinked into puddles and onto metal from eaves, wet canvas, and plastic tarps. It reminded her of music and made her heart flutter with sudden nostalgia.

Amos asked all the questions he had asked every time he came back: where were they, where were they headed, how had he died, why had she brought him back... And she answered each with the same level of dissociation she had before, except for the last question.

She stopped and looked back at him and couldn't lie. For every lie she had told in her life, a piece of herself curled inward further away from the person she once was. So, she told him: "Because I needed one of you to witness me get my retribution. And no matter how hard I try, I can't bring back Dad."

The marten paused. "I...don't understand. Your dad? How do we know each other?"

"You remember a girl, don't you?" She told him as she walked. "Peas and carrots. Singing a song."

"I..." His voice cut out. "Now that you mention it: yes. It's fuzzy. Like an old recording."

She knew this was a bad idea: letting it all spill out like this. She was so close. This was almost all over but she realized she didn't want to go through it alone. She wanted him to know what had happened. Wanted him to understand why this was so important. Not just a physical embodiment to join her in the room but a soul with knowledge of her struggle, of her fight. She wanted *him* back even if he was just a copy.

Ella sang the song, first as a hum so as not to wake the dozing occupants of the outskirts. As they parted the tents and fell into the stone path that led toward town, she began to recite the lyrics.

Soon enough, Amos hummed along.

By the time she reached the end of the stone path and saw the backs of the first houses at the edge of town, she was crying.

She turned to look at him.

"It's you," Amos's voice trembled. "You're her."

Ella nodded.

"But...who are you? And who am I? I'm not your dad. You said you couldn't bring him back. I don't understand."

"You're my *father*, Amos," she said. "And Hugh was my *dad*."

"What?" So soft. She almost hadn't heard it.

"You forgot everything: you left us and fell somewhere inside your own head. Dad took you to a clinic for treatment. They killed you and I don't think you even knew what was happening." She licked the salty tears and rubbed her cheeks to dry them.

"'They?'" The marten shook its head. "Who's 'they?' Janet, I don't..."

"Don't worry. The ones who killed you are dead. But not the one who gave the orders. He's still alive. We're going to visit him."

She turned back around and started for the houses.

"Janet," he called after her. "Wait!"

Ella softened her footsteps, her vision adjusted in the dingy morning darkness. The streetlamps in town were dim and cast woozy, rum-colored spots on the cracked pavement. The buildings stood tall along the main street, innards masked by unassuming shadowed facades.

"Please stop! Janet!" The marten's paws skittered on the road behind her.

"That isn't actually my name," she said quietly.

"It's not," Amos agreed. "But I don't know what your real name is. It doesn't matter right now because I know what it is you're here to do."

She kept walking. The house where the Man lived was spacious, that much she knew. He was a man of modernity. He liked things that were odd shapes because he had built that monstrosity in the field not for his patients but for himself. It would be a clean house, too, and white.

"Killing him won't satisfy your dad. If your dad is anything like me, it won't."

The statement stung. "You don't know how hard it was for him after we lost you. You don't know what it's like to watch one father lose their mind and then watch the other one lose their body to hunger."

The marten galloped out in front of her and spun around. "I don't. You're right. I can't imagine how difficult this world has been for you, Janet. But you are here! You have survived this long and I know you have the tenacity to keep going. But this isn't how you do it."

She narrowed her gaze at him. "How do you know? You're the twelfth copy of a man who couldn't remember I even existed when he died."

"That's not all I am to you," Amos said, his voice cracking. "Right? You said it yourself: you brought me back twelve times. You need someone to tell you this is wrong. I'm the one who's going to say it, Janet."

She clenched her teeth, trying not to scream, trying not to blow this entire moment. This wasn't how things were supposed to be. He was supposed to *understand*. Why had she said anything? She could have ignored all of his questions, snuck into the Man's house and killed him as he dreamed about God knew what and it would be over.

But she'd had to dwell on things. This place had gotten to her. *He'd* gotten to her.

She kept going. At the end of the first street where a road intersected, she saw the house. Exactly as she'd imagined. A Corinthian monolith with pillars out in front of its statuesque black door. White siding.

"You know I won't be able to do anything to stop you," Amos said behind her. "I can't possibly. All I can do is ask. Please don't."

So real. So unlike a copy.

"You don't know." She sniffed and swung her backpack off. She unzipped it and rested her hands on her shiny new wrench. "You didn't watch."

She put the pack back on and walked up the front path toward the door of the ugly house. The front steps didn't creak when she tread on them. As she grasped the ice-cold knob to the front door, it made no noise when she opened it. Ella looked back over her shoulder at the marten as it shuffled up the walk toward her and let the door creak closed.

EIGHT

The house was warm and its entry room hollow. Even in the darkness of early morning, it was too white. Shadows struck the walls in slight angles as firelight flickered from the room ahead. A fire this early in the morning? Maybe he had a lackey tending to it, stoking it to the detriment of their own sleep.

But as she approached, she saw the figure reclined in an armchair in front of the smoldering logs, a canvas bound book perched in his liver-spotted hands and knew it was him: not a servant, not a lackey. He glanced up at her over the rims of his glasses. "Ah, it's that time, is it?"

She blinked. "It's what time?"

The Man set the book down on the coffee table nearby and picked up his mostly empty whiskey glass. A skim of liquid dribbled down his throat as he knocked it back. "My execution. I've only been waiting seven years. Imagined every night a different way it would go. Some of those times, I thought it might be you if you were still alive."

She snorted. "You don't fucking know me."

"I do." His eyes had a boredom to them that set her

cheeks on fire. "Your father was a guest at my facility."

Her breath left her. "How—"

"—Or your mother. Or your grandfather. Your cousin…" He took a shuddering breath and went on. "Point is: someone you cared about was there when the world was set on fire. Someone you loved got a syringe full of drugs to put them out of their misery before you could say your goodbyes and it's taken you this long to work up the stomach to find me and even the score."

She stared at him. "You seem amused."

"No," the Man said. "I'm not. This isn't how I wanted to die. But it's better than what my own body has in store for me." He put his fingers through his hair and pulled. Clumps of greying black hair came free with ease. "Radiation therapy once a week. Does fuck all for the liver cancer without the chemo to help it."

"I'm not here to give you sympathy," she croaked. She held up the wrench.

His eyes dropped on it. "Ah. Bludgeoning. Didn't take you for a girl to get her hands dirty. But…I see the blood on your shoes. You've gotten some practice in."

Amos's voice popped into her head. "Guess you shouldn't assume. It makes an ass out of you and me."

The Man chuckled and set the empty glass down on the table. "Mind if I take a leak before you do me in? I'd rather not piss all over my carpet."

"What's it matter? It's going to be covered in your blood anyway."

"That's a good point," he said with raised eyebrows. He grunted as he got up from the armchair. It was the first time she'd seen him stand and she was surprised by how hunched over he was.

She had a memory from the hospice house years ago that wobbled and wiggled like Jello in her mind when she looked back on it: a tall, bearded man in a white coat with pomade in his hair who gazed at her and her fathers like they were nothing but rolls of quarters. He'd treated them like they were, too.

"So, do you want to ask me?"

"Ask you what?" she asked, irritation staining her tone. She adjusted her grip on the wrench. She wanted it to feel warm in her hand, for its hold and weight to feel familiar. But it was all wrong. It wasn't the same as her dad's wrench.

"Why did I do it? Why kill them all?"

"Because you didn't care about them," she snorted. "Because money is money. And you're as filthy with it as everyone else who took over a house in this town."

"Maybe," The Man said. "Maybe I was a cocky shit-heel who got in over his head, who borrowed money from the wrong people and cared more about saving his own skin than that of the people he swore an oath to help." He cocked his head. "Like your father."

She ground her teeth. "You *do* remember."

"The little girl with the two dads. Christ, you've been through the ringer, haven't you? Didn't your other daddy die on the railroad? Shorn in half when he was too starved to be able to move?"

The assertion dug its claws into her. Her grip tightened on the wrench. "Let's get this over with," she snarled.

He put up his hands and dropped them just as quickly.

"Not here. Not on my rug. Outside. That way, if you or someone else decides they want this place for themselves, they won't need to clean it first."

"Look at you being all charitable," she jeered, backing away from the doorway to let him waddle through.

They meandered up the hallway, her at the Man's back itching to bring the wrench down on his skull before they cleared the entrance way. Apprehension stymied her as did the tiny scratching sounds at the front door.

"The fuck is that noise?" the Man asked.

She heard Amos shouting on the other side but couldn't tell what he was saying. "Open it," she ordered the Man.

He did.

In the fresh warmth of the early morning, she recognized the marten huddled on the stoop, its tiny eyes staring up at them, ears flattened. "Oh, thank god," Amos whispered. "You haven't…"

"What the hell is that?" The Man scrunched up his face. "A ferret?" He kicked at it.

The marten skittered out of the way and gave a high-pitched squeal.

"It's yours, isn't it?" The Man sneered over his shoulder. "I knew your family was a bizarre one. Heard some stories about you all living outside of town. All that herbal medicine and pagan crap filling your heads and you still brought your ailing father to me for help. You still needed modern medicine?"

"And look where it got us!" The wrench rose over her head and slammed down against his right shoulder.

The man grunted and fell forward onto his knees.

The marten flung itself out of the way to avoid being crushed. "Don't!" Amos yelped.

But she was fueled now. The image of her dad's body on the tracks renewed in her mind's eye: a sight she'd sworn to herself she'd bury beneath the memories of a hundred beautiful things he'd done for her before his death. Hugh wasn't a perfect dad but he had given her everything to make sure *she* made it.

"You're going to wake everybody in town before you're through you know," the Man panted. "If you have any hopes of making it out of here alive, you'll make it quick."

"This will be quick." The words broiled on her tongue. "Quicker than you dying from cancer anyway." She swept the wrench out to the side, held it with both hands before swinging it wide like a baseball bat. The connection it made with the side of his head and jaw split the air like the sound of eggs cracking.

The Man let out a dry gasp as he flopped into the mud, holding his mouth.

The marten leapt at her pant leg, its pin-like teeth breaking through her pants and the skin of her shin. She curled her hand down around its midsection to pull it away and it sank its teeth into the fleshy web between her thumb and forefinger. She flung the marten with a hiss and it tumbled into the grass.

"Please!" Amos begged. "You don't have to kill him!"

"Yes, I do." She dropped to her knees next to the Man's flailing body. He tried to get up but she shoved him back down with both hands.

"I remember him," Amos said, his voice trembling.

She glanced at the marten. "Who?"

"Your dad. Not all of him. But pieces. And I know he was stubborn. I can still taste that…anger he made me feel when he wouldn't listen to me." He gave a sharp laugh. "He cared too much. Too much."

Ella stared. None of the animals she'd put copies of Amos's soul into had remembered Hugh. Not a whisper of him. It had taken almost no time at all for the marten to latch onto what the fox had taken hours to recollect about his memories of a daughter. Maybe he wasn't a copy at all. Maybe Amos had never been a copy…

The Man tried to get up again, his pained moans filling the air and steadily growing louder. She shoved him down once more. No. The spells she'd been taught weren't powerful enough to do that kind of thing. They couldn't…

But he remembered. He *remembered*. "Do you remember his name?" she asked him.

"No…"

A pin stuck in her hope; deflating…

The marten took a step toward her. "But I remember his compassion. He always gave to the point of exhaustion. He couldn't let anything go."

Hugh. Her dad. The man who would rather surprise her with a gift from nature or a home-cooked treat rather than have to put his foot down as a parent. Who would always let her climb into bed with them when she couldn't sleep night after night. Who never said no to strawberry French toast until there was no money to buy the ingredients and no way to make them. Amos was right. He gave and gave and gave.

"I had told him, I think, that he needed to do something for himself. He needed to let me go," Amos whispered. "But he couldn't."

No. He couldn't. She remembered that argument between them. She was supposed to have been asleep but the star-shapes on her nightlight shone too brightly and her mind whirled as she listened to them fight. Amos never raised his voice once and Hugh couldn't keep his under control. He wanted to try more concoctions, more herbs and supplements but Amos was done with them. They made him tired. They made him sick. They kept him from enjoying life and enjoying his family.

"I didn't want to go there," Amos said. "I didn't make that choice."

Something burrowed up from deep inside her chest. It clawed its way up her throat with the desperation of a person buried before they were dead, struggling under the weight of the dirt. "You're trying to distract me. I can't let you do that."

Even Amos's yell wasn't enough to keep her wrench from flying, from the fixed jaw cutting a wide gash along the back of the Man's skull. His grunts came up in bubbles in the mud as he slumped down again.

"Stop, Barbarella, stop!"

The screams quieted the roiling in her head, the kettle pulled from the burner, the whistling fading... She glanced at the marten and let the wrench drop to her side. "What did you call me?" Her tongue felt numb.

The marten shook all over. "I...don't know why I called you that. Everything is so scrambled in my head. I can't put it in order…" Amos wailed. "She's not her. Your little girl… she wouldn't do this."

A familiar tightness pressed in on her from all sides. She'd seen this before. Back when she'd brought the first animals to life, before she knew what she was really doing…

The marten flopped on its side awkwardly. "You're not real. You can't be. This is a horrible dream," Amos moaned to himself.

Nausea spilled over her. She'd heard it time after time as the creatures she'd revitalized eventually obliterated themselves with their own claws, threw themselves over long drops, ran out in front of the last remaining vehicles…

The root was pinned in a moment of time that threatened to steal the rest of the air from her lungs: the last time she saw her father. The last time he had an inkling of who she was. Her dad had wrangled her from the room as Amos had collapsed in a heap at the foot of his bed, crying that he was trapped in his own head. How eerily calm it was moments later when he forgot what he'd been doing and just stared out the windows. "Pretty view. Very striking," he'd whispered.

The marten raised its paws to its face. In the faint porch light, she noticed drops of blood and the soft tearing of fur and flesh. "I can't get out. Can't get out! Someone let me out of here!" he screamed.

Ella clambered away from the convulsing body of the Man beneath her. Her hand scooped up the animal and held it to her chest. "Shh. Shh. It's okay," her voice broke.

The animal struggled under her grip, claws raking her hands. "Get me out! Get me out!"

She held on, biting her cheek to hold back the pain of each slice through her skin. "You're okay, Amos. You're going to be okay."

The marten squealed. It bit her fingers. When it wrangled itself around in her arms, its talons sunk into her chest and razed the skin there. In a weak moment, she let go.

Spilling onto the grass, the creature bolted off into the street and disappeared around the corner.

"Amos!" she screamed after him.

A light popped on in the house next door. Then another. She realized that others had come on already in the commotion. Ella pushed herself up off the ground, scraped the wrench up from where it lay in the mud and flung herself toward the front door of the Man's house. She needed to get out of sight. Couldn't run into the street. She'd be a sitting duck.

The strangeness of the statement hit into her as she ripped open the front door and sealed herself inside the quiet house. She'd heard her father say it once. Amos had taught her all of those dumb idioms when she was small.

The thought of him cracked against the iron façade she was trying to put on. Amos. She needed to find him.

Ella plodded further into the house as the murmurs of people gathered out front and cries of alarm rose up. They'd found the Man. Still breathing. She hadn't finished the job.

She entered the room with the fireplace. The blaze had dwindled and cast ripples of orange light like waves across the carpet. Her eyes found another door that would lead to another room that would hopefully get her back outside. But she froze.

The carpet. The Man had been so damn worried about staining the carpet.

Wrestling the chair and coffee table out of the way, she peeled back a corner of the patterned rug. Nothing. She kept pulling, bringing the opposite corners together until something poked out: a manila envelope.

Dogs barked from the front of the house. She heard the whine of a warning siren building up as someone cranked it to full pitch from one of the watchtowers. She ran to the next room, skirted around the island of a kitchen and out a back screen door that slapped shut behind her.

Her lungs burned as she ran. Backyards filled with empty swimming pools, discarded lawnmowers, and derelict garden sheds loomed around her. A bygone era of the suburbs. Grassless lawns that gave way into scraggly brush that would, in turn, slope back down into the outskirts.

Sharp barks pitched into the air behind her as her lead-filled legs pushed her further into the brush. The tall weeds snagged in her hair and snatched at her exposed skin, the scrapes on her arms raging at every touch.

A high-pitched shriek filled the sky followed by louder barking. The shriek abruptly cut off. Oxygen left her as she kept running; as her entire chest cracked. She wanted to scream his name.

She followed a small gully, boots scaling the rocks until she found the end, and climbed the drainpipe up out. Far behind her, the lingering shouts of people calling their dogs back settled her mind into a faint ease of safety. But failure was close behind and on its heels was shame.

Ella crossed the dirt path at the edge of town into the

outskirts once more, the warning siren like a harbinger at her back. Even as morning light dredged her, she didn't stop until she met the train tracks again. Once there, she followed them back, feet sore and body begging for rest.

Not until she saw the overgrown path did she flee the railroad. Another mile stretched between her and her destination. She hugged the folder to her like a life preserver every step of the way and focused on her feet, on the scuffles of her boots in the dirt. Whenever an errant thought surfaced, she pushed it back down. Dirt and boots. Dirt and boots.

The hospice house welcomed her in the morning light differently than it had the previous day. As she crossed its empty parking lot and opened the front door to its waiting room once more, she let the dirt and the boots fade. She laid across the floor and closed her eyes.

Sleep found her with the brightness of the sun soaking her in its warmth.

NINE

Ella didn't awake until night.

The hush of it unearthed a new peace that was oddly comforting. She wandered the hall of the home down to the pool room and the showers and out the back door.

The moon etched long shadows of the crosses across the faded grass. She took a step toward it and movement in the stalks froze her.

A fox, scrawny and rust-colored, emerged.

"Amos?" His name fell from her lips.

It stared at her without moving and didn't speak.

"Foxes are clever," Amos had told her as a child when he gave her the tiny fox figurine. "They know things. Slippery little guys who can survive just about anything. Loyal, too."

"You think any of them will make it?" she'd asked. It had been a month without rain. They used to see them on their daily walks. Then, not one.

"I do. After all, they're magic."

The fox sniffed into the wind and bounded away into the grass.

She took a deep breath in through her nose and let

the memories in. She let her parents' voices in to whisper her goodnights like they had when they were alive. Sanely. Tenderly.

TEN

The old house did not welcome her. It was a skeleton with flecks of its former life clinging to it like flesh to a desiccated corpse. Instead, she welcomed herself into it. Reintroduced and made herself familiar with its new identity.

She scooped the last of the pond water into her jug and didn't think about how it used to look when she was smaller. She found birthday candles in the drawers of the old hutch where her parents' used to keep all the party decorations. An old lighter remained in one of the drawers, too, with a bit of butane still preserved inside.

Ella had braved the basement of the hospice house with the light of day to return to should she need it. She'd found the old belongings. She'd found her father's book of poetry, his glasses, one of his favorite shirts…

In the living room, she placed the candles. She poured the bit of pond water and laid out the wildflowers and dried herbs from the field Amos had been buried in. She opened the book of poetry and found the one she remembered the best, the one she'd had tattooed on her by some kid who didn't know what any of it had meant. She read it:

"Think of asters,
Think of daisies,
Think of cosmos,
In the fields far and wide.
Think of the night,
Of its hallowed heart
Nestled amongst the stars in the sky.
I am there with you always,
My darling Ella."

Lastly, she cried over the bones of her father and waited in the dark for signs of life.

ACKNOWLEDGEMENTS

Inspiration comes from a lot of strange places sometimes. So, here are some strange thank yous that might not make sense to you, the reader, but are necessary regardless:

To Jose Gonzalez. Your music is the exact mood that this book is. Thanks for making it.

To Stanley Tucci, Colin Firth, and Bleecker Street for making *Supernova*. If you haven't seen it: watch it.

To Stevie Nicks. The seed of this idea sprouted while listening to you sing.

To Cormac McCarthy for writing *The Road*.

To the horror community for believing in this story when all you had to go on was a cover and a synopsis.

To the early readers: you are awesome.

To you for taking the dive in.

Thank you.

photo by Colin Borowske 2024

Katherine Silva is an ace Maine horror author, a connoisseur of coffee, and victim of cat shenanigans. Her favorite flavors of the genre mix grief and existentialism which she combines with her love of the New England wilderness in her works. She is a two-time Maine Literary Award finalist for speculative fiction and a member of the Horror Writers of Maine, The Horror Writers Association, and New England Horror Writers Association. Katherine is also editor-in-chief of Strange Wilds Press. You can find out all about her work at katherinesilvaauthor.com.

Milton Keynes UK
Ingram Content Group UK Ltd.
UKHW010820220424
441551UK00005B/379